DONUT HOLES
Sticky Pieces of Fictionalized Realities

by
Matty Stanfield

For Byron Kim,

With a love and thanks, infinite
...my reason.

Special Thanks to:
Alan Kropp, Dr. Regina Marshall, Jenny Angelo, Beth Iglecia,
Aaron Howe, Iris Stanfield, Roy Stanfield, Edna Gertrude
Stanfield, Donna Mullen, Kathy Artlip, Kathryn Patrice Freeman,
Damian Ryan, Ingrid Hawkinson, Gina Betcher
Jennifer Stewart, Angie Szeto, Darren Stein, Lola
and Little Bagel.

Also, a very special thanks to the writing and inspiration of
Mattilda Bernstein Sycamore.

And finally, Ms. Barbra Streisand, who unknowingly got me
through the darkest moments of my life...and continues to do so.

Credits:

Cover Photograph:
Roy Stanfield
http://mmmmmmmmmmmmmimic.net

Cover and Interior Design:
Byron B. Kim
byronkim@gmail.com

Quote from "Prince Charming"
Written by Adam Ant and Marco Pirroni
Available on "Prince Charming" by Adam and the Ants, Epic Records
Used by permission of BMG Music Publishing LTD.

Quote from "Storms"
Written by Stevie Nicks
Available on "Tusk" by Fleetwood Mac, Warner Bros. Records
Used by permission of Welsh Witch Music.

ISBN 1442151919
EAN-13 9781442151918

April 2009
Matty Stanfield
glittercrush@gmail.com
www.matty03.wordpress.com

Contents...

Introduction:
Sticky Pieces...

I do not fancy myself a writer.

I studied literature and creative writing throughout school and college. I would sit in writing courses, working on a single story for weeks on end only to receive criticism that my work was unfocused and illogical in the use of grammar.

I don't like rules. I like to break them. This includes grammar. Yes, I know the golden rules of the English language both written and spoken. I simply reject these rules. I reject all the rules across the board. This was the main reason my university advisor and professor expressed such relief when I decided that teaching was not for me.

This professor, a dear person and an inspiration, once told me that my writing flowed out as a sort of jazz riff. Further to the point, she indicated that my writing seemed to have just leapt from my brain on to the page. What was my hurry? I was not in a hurry. This was and is just how I write.

I never take offense at criticism or feedback, but I do become weary when I consistently receive the same sort that seems to reflect a relevant concern. These concepts escape me and I have learned I have no control over certain aspects of my style. And, I have decided to simply embrace it.

I used to write the truth about what had either happened to me or situations that I had observed in the manner of a journalist. Changing only the names, I felt this was the best way to convey my perceived experiences.

There is no real truth...just perceptions of what is true to each of us. However, I quickly discovered that the facts of my life seemed entirely fictional to readers. So, I began to tone things down. My realities became fictionalized to become more palatable for the reader.

The order of my stories may seem illogical or confusing. It is a conscious and deliberate decision on my part to strip away any real sense of chronological order.

So, here you have a collection of some of my stories. Sticky fictionalized reality. That is how I would term these stories or pieces

Speaking strictly for myself, life is a mess. It is a chronic journey of joy, mistake, love, anger, confusion, pain, bliss, ugliness and beauty all experienced at once. And, in varying degrees of dose and intensity, I push forward through the wreckage of my life with curiosity, humor, horror, love and hope.

I do not think of my life in a linear way. To be honest, I don't think in a linear manner. Therefore, I felt it fitting that the order of my "stories" be random. If, at times, you feel a bit confused or disoriented as you read then I have accomplished what I set out to do.

Not to go all Forrest Gump on your ass, I do think that life is a bit like a bag or box of donut holes. Messy, sticky, at times sickeningly sweet; other times minus much flavor, mixed-up, too soft, too hard, just right, juicy, dry, and mysterious flavors. While one consumes life there is often a seeming miss of a whole. Fragmented and in pieces – life comes assorted,

confused and a bit too filling. There doesn't seem to be enough of it. And, yet, there is somehow never enough.

I can't just eat one. I crave another.

No matter how delicious one piece (or experience) might be, I always anticipate another to be stale as I sink my teeth into the moment. So, I continue on through the assortment longing for delicious fulfillment.

This is the confusion and bargain bin center of life. It is easier served in pieces removed from the whole. When it becomes too much, the bag or box can be resealed and placed in a safe place until I am ready to venture for another bite.

I have resisted the urge, when at all possible, to provide specific dates, times or places. Whether the situations or experiences occur in a small town in Texas or in New York, Boston and San Francisco. Whether I am a child, young adult or lost adult...they all come together. They are packaged in a random bunch as an assorted baker's dozen – give or take a few.

The donut holes (or stories) can be eaten in the order as they appear or as one may choose to eat (or read) as the fingers lead. It will not matter.

I can't speak for anyone but myself, but no matter the method applied to eating (or reading) I find it difficult to form a complete meal. For me, meals like art are without end. The words go on. I reach for them –- messy, soft, hard, moist or so dry they crumble before I can even delivery them to my senses....donut holes are not always easily digested.

Matty Stanfield
April 2009

"...don't you ever
Lower yourself
Forgetting all your standards
Don't you ever lower yourself
Forgetting all your standards

Prince Charming
Ridicule is nothing to be scared of
Don't you ever, don't you ever
Stop being dandy
Showing me you're handsome

Silk or leather or a feather
Respect yourself
And all of those around you..."

Adam & The Ants

"...I'd like to leave you with something warm
But never have I been a blue calm sea
I have always been a storm..."

Stevie Nicks

THE DINGO ATE MY BABY!!!!

"Sir? Are you OK?"...

Was I okay? It was a good question. I was slouched on the floor of a hallway in some old San Francisco government

building. I was just outside the restroom where I had just lost my "attempt" at lunch. Exhausted and feeling faint I had decided to slide down the wall and catch my breath. However, instead of catching it I lost it. That was when the crying jag began.

I just sat on the floor in my father's-far-too-big-for-me-brown-leather-coat and cried. Mom had made it through the surgery but I had been told that we wouldn't know about the cancer for another 48 hours. But, they think they got it all and caught it in time. This was a relief and the most important thing going. But, I felt spent. The crying had stopped and, somewhat dazed, was getting it together when the security guy had approached me.

"I'm fine."

But, as he pointed out, I was on the wrong floor. I had to go up to the 19th floor where my bag and coat were inspected. I had to remove my belt, shoes, all items in my pockets, bracelet and monkey penis necklace to get thru the sensor without beeping. Once I was "cleared" I gathered my stuff, put on my shoes and took another elevator up to the 22nd floor.

This was the day I have been dreading since Christmas Eve. But at least this would be the end of one of the most humiliating bits of my journey: Bankruptcy.

Trust me. It could happen to you. No matter what you think. Cast no judgments. It can happen and it fucking sucks. The bankruptcy filing was back in November and no one contested at the official California Meeting of Creditors where they are to stake their claim against my filing. I was so relieved.

My cheap lawyer told me that I was all set and could really get a fresh start rolling. But on Christmas Eve he called me to let me know that American Express was filing lawsuit against

4

me to contest their portion of my bankruptcy. And, the court date was already set for March 17th at 2:30 PM.

Deep breathe. I entered the Room 22 and discovered that I was in an actual formal court room complete with jury box, microphones, video cameras, seats, an elaborate judges' desk, two opposing tables with mics and an intimidating podium with two microphones. I took a seat. I sat quietly and tried to focus as my mind raced. Lawyers in suits whispered strategies and the rest of us just looked frightened. This was like a movie set for some tightly staged courtroom melodrama.

And, for some reason I found myself thinking of Meryl Streep in a bad wig pleading for mercy from a mean judge, "I swear! The dingo's took my baby! I would never hurt my baby! It was the dingos! The dingo took my baby!!!!"

Meryl's wig goes askew. Her husband's eyes fill with chemical tears. The judge looks uncomfortable. Meryl stands indignant because we know the truth. She did no wrong. The dingo ate her baby. Sadly, they left that odd black wig on her head that seemed to change positions between every cut.

For a brief minute I find myself fighting the urge to rush the podium and scream about how the dingo's fucked me over and American Express was an evil corporate empire more concerned with my little debt that the millions that they allow major corporations to scam on every day. It was the dingos and AmEx, dammit!

My proto-soap-box-courtroom-drama fantasy was crushed by the call for everyone to stand as the judge entered.

And there he was. This was the judge who was to decide my fate. Dressed in a big black gown with very little hair. I am not paranoid. He looked at those of us who were not wearing lawyer suits with disdain.

My case was called first.

"Case of American Express vs Matthew Stanfield."

I was told to approach the podium. I felt so sick. I couldn't decide if I was going to hurl or cry. What fucked up thing did I do in my last life to plunge me into these last four years? I got a grip and told myself to fuck the pity and just pretend I was tough enough to deal with this bullshit.

I looked around for the 'opposing counsel' as they are want to be called.

Suddenly, as if the voice of God was calling to me, the mean lawyer representing AmEx started speaking over the speaker system. The motherfucker phoned it in. I imagined him sitting in his multi-million dollar home playing on his home PC while he pretended to work from home.

"Your honor, Mr. Stanfield failed to file a motion to my client's claim."

Huh?

Before I could think or say anything the judge spoke, "No, I have Mr. Stanfield's motion in front of me. It was filed and it appears that it was mailed to both our court and to your office in Sacramento."

"No, your honor. We did not receive it."

My voice came out surprisingly strong, "Yes, you did. I confirmed with your administrative assistant. I have her name, the date I spoke with her and her confirmation to me written right here." I read it all into the microphones. I could hear my voice booming thru the giant room.

The judge spoke to the voice of the evil corporate lawyer and asked him to confirm if that person was his administrative assistant. The lawyer confirmed that she was but must have

been covering the phones from New York as that is where she is based. What the fuck? Then the asshole lawyer said that she was incorrect my motion had not been received.

The judge told me that I would need to resend the motion to the Sacramento office and we would reschedule the trial for April 28th at 2:30 PM.

"Thank you, your honor" said the lawyer's voice.

I fought the urge to ask if I could simply call in from work on the 28th as well. I fought the urge to say that the case should be dismissed on the grounds that AmEx wasted California funds by not making their claim at the appointed Meeting Of The Creditors and by lying when his assistant confirmed that they had received my motion back in January. I fought the urge to scream that I was going to counter-sue for putting me through great mental stress.

Instead, I leaned in and asked the judge how I could be sure to know that the lawyer would receive one after I spent the money to recopy all of the paper records. Should I send via Fed Ex or registered mail?

Before anyone could answer, I read the address info I had for the law firm to ensure I had the right info and asked for an administrative contact at the Sacramento office who might answer the phone and confirm information correctly so that I could avoid dragging this personal hell out any longer than it had already been dragged out by AmEx. This got a few laughs from the other poor non-lawyer souls sitting behind me.

I had noticed that AmEx was suing eight other people that day. Among the eight, I was the only white guy. The other seven were all people of color who looked to have about $10 all combined. Toss me in and we could have maybe sprung for a Big Mac meal. Regular sized.

I fought the urge to hiss, "You evil motherfuckers are ruining our lives!" But, I simply waited for answers. I was told to simply mail standard US mail and it would be received.

The judge looked at me as if I was a four-year-old child who had just broken Grandma's favorite coffee cup. I leaned forward and spoke, "I don't mean to be sarcastic or rude, but that is what I did in December and I even confirmed with the law office and they told me it was received. I am confused."

The invisible lawyer said it was never received. The judge told me that I needed to step down and return on April 28th. He then suggested that I hire a lawyer. I looked at him and asked, "With what? I don't have any money to hire a lawyer. I just got a new job and their first payroll check bounced. I am broke." I think I might have said something else. I can't remember. All I know is that the judge stopped me.

Then he essentially dismissed me and then *fucking thanked* the lawyer floating on some conference speakerphone system.

As I walked out, a sweet looking woman who was on the side waiting to be sued winked at me. I walked into the hallway. I wanted to cry. But, you know what? In the end none of this really matters.

My mom pulled through the surgery. I am healthy. I've got great friends. This is only money and if the California Bankruptcy Court decides that AmEx can own me then so be it. You can only get so much blood from a stone. I'm fine.

However, at this moment, I am not sure how I feel about the state of affairs in my country; a country run by corporate interests; a place where an empire like Enron can do whatever it wants; a country where the vice-president can shoot his friend and not even bother to visit him in the hospital; a place where war is the leading money maker; a country in which citizens and other human lives are expendable for a buck; a

place where I am a second class citizen just by the nature of my sexuality; a society that undervalues women because they are not men; my country of birth; a place where a corporate entity can play with your life with a conference call and the judge treats you as if you are a fucking idiot.

At that moment, I was ashamed to be a US citizen. I was angry.

I rushed from the vile building with the urge to burn a US flag and scream "Viva Revolution!"

But, my bus was just arriving. Well, so much for revolution. One must have priorities.

NOT A WORD

He didn't say a word...

My neck was sore. His big hand was firmly wrapped around my neck and had been pushing me forward. The grass was wet

and cold to my bare feet. We were now to the ditch, which separated our property from the railroad tracks. I could feel the train approaching but I wasn't able to hear it. His hand was still on my neck and I was forced to turn to the left. He shined the flashlight on the rabbit in that cage. I could now hear the train. The light from the engine was showing and the ground was shaking.

I heard the click of his pistol. I shut my eyes but knew better than to fight his hand. I was not able to turn away but I refused to watch it happen. My toes clinched into the grass blades. I formed my hands into fists and held them close to my sides. I didn't want him to see me shake.

The train was speeding past us and the thud on the tracks seemed unbearable. Of course, nothing was as loud as the shot of his pistol. It made me jump. I didn't want to look but something required me to open my eyes. I let the tears roll down my cheeks. My vision cleared a bit and snot ran over my mouth.

The rabbit's body twitched as if it was trying to find a way to jump out of the cage. The head was gone. Or, rather, it was splattered all over the cage. Too much red – I shut my eyes.

I knew what was next. I tried to break my fall with my fists, but the grass was soft. My eyes were shut so tight I could see colors dancing on the inside of my eyelids. I tried to focus on the shapes. Anything to not think about what was happening.

There it was.

It was on my back pushing me further into the grass. The end of the barrel was so hot it burned. I pushed myself into the grass in an attempt to get away from that burn. I could smell the gunpowder all around me.

11

It was quiet now except for the ringing in my ears from the shot. Dad's breath smelled of the drink that came in the blue velvet bag. I knew better than to throw up. I was trying to swallow it back down and breath at the same time. It wasn't working. But, he lay on top of me. He was crushing me. I didn't need to throw up anymore. I just held my breath. And, then the pain came.

How much time had past? It was still dark. He was carrying me back to the house. I felt like I was in some horrible nightmare.

My underwear felt wet. I was numb but I knew I'd be sore in the morning. Wasn't this a school night?

He leaned me against the frame of the house. The water from the hose was cold but felt good as it washed over my backside. Everything seemed to tingle. Then came the towel that smelled funny. Everything smelled wrong.

He pulled my legs up one at a time and pulled a new pair of underwear on me. He picked me up. A few steps and we were back in the house. I knew not to say a thing or make any sounds. Dad put me back in my bed.

As always, nothing was said.

In the morning I begged Mom to let me stay home. My stomach hurt. She refused and told me to stop acting and be a big boy. I limped to the car. It hurt to sit, but I just bit my lip.

Later I would ask for the bathroom pass. I broke out into a cold sweat as I tried to endure the pain of going to the bathroom. That pain was back. The very same pain, but now my stomach as well. I knew to push forward against the stall and turned my head down. Otherwise I knew I might fall off the seat. We could all be in trouble if I woke up on the floor again. I knew that.

The pain was going away. Now, I was just aching. I didn't want to look, but I had to see what I had deposited into the bowl. It was stringy lines of blood and some shit. I threw up and then flushed it away.

I pulled my pants back up. I was afraid to try and wipe. I pushed my face under the running water of the sink. I wasn't sweating anymore. I was relieved that no one had been in the boy's room this time.

I did my best not to limp as I walked back to class. Mrs. Phillips wanted to know why I was wet. I placed the bathroom pass back on her desk. I bit my lip and slipped back into my seat. She went on with her lesson.

The pain would come in pangs. The horrible sensation would make me cringe and bite further into my lip. It felt good to draw blood. Mrs. Phillips would ask me why I bit my lip. I would tell her it was an accident.

These pangs of pain and fear still follow me today. And, quite often, the scents and tastes of all that torture come back to me. No mouthwash or cologne can mask them. A residue called "trauma" that seems to have no restraint.

I remember the moment I gave up. Or, rather, stood up. Not too long after that night, I watched another headless rabbit trying to escape the cage. I could not face him.

Him.

My father.

But, I remember the anger welling up inside of me instead of vomit. I remember shaking away from the clutch of his giant hand. I remember telling him to go ahead and shoot my head off. I remember looking up and telling him that I would tell if he hurt me again. With clenched fists I dared my father to hurt me or kill me like the rabbits.

We started the walk back to the house. His hand came around my neck and he stopped me. I could no longer help it. I started to cry. His hand tightened. He was hurting me. My knees started to give. I fell to the ground and started to throw up.

He picked me up. His grip warned me not to make any noises, but a sound was coming from inside me as I tried to not choke.

The light of the bathroom blinded me. I felt a wet cloth wiping my feet, knees, back and chest. I heard the cloth slam against the tile walls. I didn't dare look at him.

His hand came back around my neck. He turned my head down and forced me to look at the cabinet beneath the sink. His boot opened the door to the little cabinet. He placed the pistol next to the Comet. The door shut. He squeezed my neck. He didn't say a word to me, but he called to Mom – "Babe, the kid's sick! I can't deal with the puke! Get your ass in here!"

I got on the floor and put my head against the toilet. He walked out of the bathroom. I heard my mother ask him what was going on. I heard her ask him a lot of things. I can't remember him answering her. I think he just ignored her and said nothing.

Mom sat on the floor next to me. "Sweetie. No need to cry. It's just a virus."

I said nothing. As a child, I never did.

DONUT HOLES

I didn't have a choice. It had been decided....

My father had already arranged it all through one of his pals. Besides, as he pointed out, I needed a job and it would

help me to secure that Texas Hardship Drivers License. My parents wanted me to have that license so I could pick up my baby brother from day care and run errands. I wanted it so I could have a car and be the ultimate in cool.

The car, a 1966 Buick, had already been secured. It was parked in the garage. A former neighbor's husband had killed himself in the back seat. My father purchased it from the widow for fifty dollars. I had only had to clean the crud in the back. Now, all that remained was a stain. I told my friends I didn't know what it was if they asked. It tends to freak your people out if they discover that they are sitting where some depressed old man blew his brains out. I also had discovered it freaked people out even more than I had cleaned up dried brain matter from a car.

I always suspected that my father was not telling me the truth. I always thought that the widow might have paid him to remove it from her drive way. I didn't care. I only had to pay him fifty dollars and the car was mine. My parents pledged to pay the insurance for me. I learned the hard way that we never had car insurance. My father simply photocopied a 'doctor'd up' old insurance card. It worked for a number of years.

No matter. It was my car and I needed that license to drive it. I would be eligible in November when I turned fourteen. And, having a job would only help me secure the right to have it. For now, I would need to depend upon my mother, her mother and the wife of one of my father's pals to pick me up.

I had already discovered drugs. I also saw this potential job as a way to score more weed due to the fact that I would be making money. Little did I know that would be taking an unexpected boon of a turn. So, even though I would be the only person my age I knew who would have a job I decided it was going to be a good thing. Besides, I had no choice or say in the matter.

I was to work at a tiny donut shop. I had noticed it a couple of times over the last couple of years. My father's pal's son had worked there very briefly. He told my parents that the couple that owned it were a little eccentric but good people.

Located in a rather shifty side of town and adjacent to a very low-income mobile home community. I had never even thought of venturing in, as it looked filthy. And it was, but it was not really so much a donut shop as a front for a small time drug running business. The shop allowed the owners to run drugs and hide the money made. It didn't take me long to figure it all out.

Marla, the actual owner, was skeptical toward me at first. She taught me how to operate the register, how to package the donuts and the various duties she expected me to carry out every day. I worked three hours every day during the week and six hours on Saturdays. After my first day Marla moved herself to the back of the store that housed the kitchen and the office. The back could be seen from the counter and serving area.

Jerry, her husband, was seldom there. My understanding was that he opened the store very early in the morning and made the day's supply of donuts, but was gone by eight in the morning. Clifford would then arrive to relieve Jerry for the rest of the day. Clifford was Marla's ex-husband. The three of them were always fighting but I found them to be the most exciting and cool group of adults I had yet to know.

After my first week, Marla announced that I was on my own. She gave me the key and warned me not to "fuck" anything up or steal any money. She made a point of reminding me that Clifford would be in the back till about five every evening.

I remember asking her what Clifford was doing back there as Jerry made all the donuts in the morning. If we ran out of donuts, we simply ran out of them. No more were made

excepting on Saturdays when Clifford would make a new batch at Noon. There were not many donut shoppers during the afternoon while I was there...just lots of calls on the phone for Clifford. Marla declined to give me a real answer to my question and advised me to just focus on the customers. I was only to go in the back as the duties required. I was advised to give Clifford his space and just to call to him from the front if he got any calls. I was to put them on hold. Then call back to Clifford.

Looking back on it I would guess that Clifford was in his early to mid thirties. He had the look of a late 70's stoner who was probably hot at one point but was now burnt out and sporting a large beer belly which always managed to be exposed from under his OP t-shirts. He seemed to take pride in his big hairy belly. He would sometimes wear muscle shirts that were cut a bit too short. His right arm was covered in tattoos. And, I quickly came to understand that his cut-off jean shorts and flip-flops formed his signature look. One of my girlfriends who used to come by the shop thought he looked like a reject from the Village People. With his handlebar mustache her remark was not far off the money.

He had always been quiet around me. I would hear him yell at Marla in the back about her cheating him out of this or that. Or, the few times I had been around when Jerry was there I would hear Clifford warning Jerry not to turn his back on "the bitch" and Jerry would threaten to kick his ass. That would usually end in a near fistfight. I would just sit at the front enjoying the excitement of it all. Cool men fighting over stupid things. I was in teenage heaven.

Jerry, Marla's husband, was not someone you would want to mess with. Over six feet tall and muscular, he was an imposing figure. He would have been good looking except that he always seemed to be suffering with Bell's Palsey on his face. It affected his speech so he didn't talk all that much. Marla had told me to just be cool around Jerry and things would be fine.

It was my second week at the counter. I was bored. As per usual, we had no customers. This was just as well as we only had a few cream filled donuts left. I had wiped the counter about twelve times in a half hour period. I was starting to count the minutes to the time when my mother would pick me up.

"Matty, come back here I need to show you somethin'!"

This was really the first time Clifford had ever talked directly to me. I put down the rag and pushed through the swinging door that separated the bright yellow serving area from the dark kitchen and office.

I found Clifford sitting on the glaze table. His hairy legs were spread out in a rather inappropriate way. A roach was burning on a saucer next to him and a bottle of beer was next to that. He was wearing his sunglasses. His shirt was off. It was hot back there and the air was far too sweet with the mixture of pot and sugar. I asked him what was up. He offered me a rather sinister laugh.

He asked me to bring him one of the cream filled donuts. The display case was totally open and exposed to the back of the store. Feeling a bit worried but more curious than anything, I turned around, picked up a powdered cream filled donut, walked over and handed it to him.
I could see my reflection in his mirror sunglasses. They were the mirror type. Clifford slipped his middle finger in and out of the donut. His finger was covered in the cheap sugar cream Marla stocked. He slipped his finger in his mouth and sucked the cream off. I found myself wanting to laugh as he got cream on his mustache but failed to notice.

I knew he was trying to be somehow sexy or sexual. Was Clifford gay? How should I react?

"So, how do you like to get off?"

19

"What do you mean?"

"Ah, man! Come on! How do you jerk your meat off, dude?"

"I don't really do that."

Laughing, Clifford held up the donut and said that he didn't believe me. He then told me he wanted to show me something really cool but wanted to make sure I was up for it and that I could be an adult about it. He told me it would be really uncool for me to tell anyone what he was about to show me. He wanted to know if I was down with it. Could I dig from where he was coming? His 70's speak amused me.

"Sure. I'm cool."

Clifford unbuttoned his far-too-tight-fitted cut off jeans. He slipped off the table and pulled out his fully erect cock. I was shocked, but did my best to not act like it. I had started my sexual journey of self-discovery that would not fully disclose itself as gay until I would be in my senior year of high school. However, I knew I was gay. I just wasn't ready to give my desires a name. And, in an oddly funny way, this all seemed kind of "hot."

I wasn't wearing cut-offs but my 501's were tight as was the style. I had a hard on and I did not want him to know. I was relieved it was dark back there. I remember clearing my throat in an attempt to not register any excitement at what I was seeing.

Nothing of the moment had really sunk in other than I was amazed at the size of Clifford's cock. His was also the first one I had seen hard in the flesh. It was bigger than the ones I had seen in the dirty magazines my father kept hidden in his gun cabinet.

I think I was looking a bit too much at Clifford's penis because he laughed and proceeded to tell me that he had gotten a hard watching my two "little" girlfriends who had just come in. He asked if I enjoyed the little girls flirting with me. I told him that I didn't think that they were flirting. I told him that they were just friends and that we had been playing around. He told me that he would love to play with their little tits but not enough to risk going to jail. He asked me if I had sucked on their "little titties"

I gave some nervous lame answer in hopes of sounding cool and fitting in. I decided that Clifford was not gay. He was just into thirteen-year-old girls. Gross.

But, then things took a turn. He asked me if I was queer. I said no. He told me that he wasn't so sure judging by the bulge in my jeans. I felt flushed and afraid.

He asked me if I thought his dick was big. I remember trying to be funny and asking him if we were on some form of "Hi! Your On Porn Hidden Camera." He laughed and told me he liked me. He leaned forward and added that he liked me a lot. He then told me that he was going to show me a secret that would bring me more pleasure than any pussy or any hot bitch mouth.

Clifford began to fuck the donut with his cock. I really could not decide what it was I should be doing. Part of me wanted to run away in sheer horror and another wanted to stay and watch. So, I stayed in place watching while attempting not to appear shocked.

He was tearing the donut up. The crumbs and cream were all over not only his dick but also the floor beneath him. Even still, I decided I didn't mind the idea of mopping it up. I was curious to see what was going to happen. Would a dick that big shoot more cum than mine? And, would it matter that he was an actual man. It seemed to matter in the dirty videos that I had seen. I didn't shoot that much cum.

Clifford managed to reach up with his left hand between thrusts and pushed his sunglasses off. They fell to the floor. He didn't seem to care. He stared into my eyes. I didn't know what to do. He proceeded to tell me that it was really getting him off looking at me as he fucked the donut. He shot his load all over his torn up donut and hands. It spilled on to the floor. There was a lot, but it didn't shoot as far as I was thinking it might. In fact, it didn't really shoot as much as spray. However, it made quite the mess.

He cocked his head to the side and asked me to really tell him how I got off. I began to laugh and told him not with donuts. He then put the abused donut in his mouth and ate it. He licked the cum, sugar cream and donut off his fingers. Clifford suggested I take a bite next time. I wish I could remember what I said but I essentially declined and told him I had to go back to the front. I remember his smile. I remember thinking it funny that he thought he was sexy. Still. There was no denying that I had quite a hard on. However, I told myself he had little to do with it. It was just exciting to see a hard dick come. Donut or not – I was impressed. But, I kept telling myself I was not impressed with Clifford.

As I locked the door, closed the big donut light and turned the sign to "closed" Clifford walked into the front area and asked me if I wanted to get stoned. I told him that my mom would be there any minute. But, it didn't take much convincing to get me back into the kitchen to take a few tokes with him. Under his breath he muttered that he should have offered me a "J' before pulling out his cock. I remember laughing as he slipped his flip flops off and smeared the crumbs, sugar and cum on the floor. He teased me and told me to lick it all up. I told him to dream on.

I freaked when I heard my mom's car horn. Clifford laughed, gave me a piece of gum and told me to be cool. As my mother pulled out of the parking lot I watched Clifford open the front door of the shop and let in about six black guys. I

had seen one of them hanging around the mobile home park. He was a dealer. Mom told me I smelled funny. I ignored her and reached over and played with my little brother who was strapped into his baby seat and trying to escape.

A week or so later Marla marched into the store. I had only been there for about an hour so it was not even close to time to shut down. She walked passed me as if I did not exist. She and Clifford began to fight almost instantly and I heard her slap him. There was a long exchange of expletives and Clifford slammed through the swinging door so hard I thought it was going to fly off its hinges. He didn't say goodbye. He just stormed out of the shop and his corvette peeled out of the parking lot.

Marla walked into the serving area. She was brushing her hair. She smelled good. She told me to call my mom and tell her that her boss would drive me home, as it was time for my review. I wasn't sure what a "review" was at that point in life. After I made the call, Marla closed the shop early and told me that we were going to let the daily duties fuck off. She then had me accompany her to into the back office. She informed me that she and I were going to get stoned together.

I was thrilled. As we smoked she began to tell me that she remembered what it was like to be thirteen. She promised me that it got better. I laughed. I was definitely getting a nice buzz on. I felt that this was one of the coolest moments of my life. I was in a closet of an office, which also featured a door leading to the dirtiest toilet in southeast Texas getting stoned with my boss who smelled of expensive perfume. So fucking cool.

She told me that she was 26. Thinking back on it I think she was trying to tell me that she was young but she seemed like an old lady to me. She asked me if I wanted to see her "boobs." She was pulling her halter-top down before I could answer. I remember thinking it was kind of neat. I had never been close to a woman's exposed breasts before. They were kind of small but she had perfect pink nipples. I remember

thinking that she looked better than the porn actresses who graced Dad's Hustler and Penthouse magazines.

Marla was literally putting out heat from her body. She was practically on me. I was leaning against the wall and she was starting to lean in to me. We were the same height. She commented that this and my tan arms were making her wet. I wasn't exactly sure what that meant, but I did have an idea. I decided that it had to do with either her pussy or her butt hole. And, I knew that being wet must be a good thing.

Marla instructed me to play with her "boobs" and told me that I could suck on them if I wanted. I was enjoying the high and looking at her tits but I felt odd about the idea of actually touching them. And, the idea of sucking on them made me feel really uncomfortable. But, I was curious. I touched her left breast. It was so soft, but this action was ruining my high. I took a long drag on the joint. I was determined to try and play it cool. I held the smoke in as far down and for as long as I could. I blew the smoke out and said no. I think I actually stuttered that I didn't want to play with her breasts.

Without missing a beat, she asked me if I was queer. I tried my best not to cough or react. I remember shrugging and saying that I wasn't sure. There was an awkward silence at this point. She took the joint and just looked at me as if assessing my worth. Under the pressure I told her that I thought I was probably gay but that I didn't see much point in talking about it as I was stuck in the hell of Texas. This made her laugh. She commented that this was a smart move on my part.

Marla pulled her halter-top back up to cover her 'boobs' and began to ask me if I liked working for she and Jerry. I told her I loved it and couldn't wait 'til I could start driving my car and maybe working more on Saturdays to make some extra money. She seemed quite pleased.

I told her I had a cool friend who also needed a job. I assured her that my friend partied. It turned out she knew her mother. Marla told me that she didn't think it would be a good idea for her to hire the daughter of one of her best customers. My cool factor slipped as I told her that Abby's mom didn't eat food much less donuts. I went on, in that way one does when one is stoned, that Abby's mother was always starving herself and was an anorexic. The problem was I could not think of the term. I think I said that Abby's mother was an asthmatic. Marla rolled her eyes and told me that she didn't sell Abby's mom donuts.

"I supply her with weed and speed."

"Oh."

While we were bonding I felt the need to tell her about Clifford and the cream filled donuts. It was happening a lot and I was getting 'creep'd' out by it. Marla shook her head.

"Cliff is such a fucking dork. I know all about that shit. He called us up and told us all about it the first time he did it in front of you. He's harmless, but I will have Jerry talk to him. I don't want him bothering my star employee!"

With that, Marla gave me a soft open mouth kiss and breathed a hit of grass down into my throat. It was kind of hot, even if she was an old lady.

I expressed my concern that her talking to Jerry would piss Clifford off. Again, she rolled her eyes and told me not to worry about it. She assured me that Clifford would not give me any grief and that he was terrified of Jerry. I remember her laughing and adding that he was also terrified of her.

I asked her if Clifford was gay. She ignored the question, but added that I didn't want to get caught up in that shit. She said something about ACDC. I remember telling her that I

didn't care too much for that band. I think she laughed and told me I was fried.

We then sat on top of Jerry's desk and talked some more. We talked mostly about Stevie Nicks and how much we both loved her. Marla leaned in really close and told me that it was her life's goal to get stoned with Stevie and that she was determined that she would be able to make that dream come true. I asked her how, but I don't think she heard me. She started singing one of the songs from the *Bella Donna* record. I remember telling her that she had a really pretty singing voice and she told me that this really meant I was fried.

After another hour or so of further talking about music and art Marla announced that it was time for us to get going. She then told me that I was getting a fifty-cent increase. I remember thinking that this seemed like a big jump at the time. But, she must have thought it wasn't much because she reminded me to keep in mind that I was being paid under the counter.

I heard the front door of the shop unlocking and opening. I turned and Marla told me it was just Jerry with "some people" "Just business" she explained. She led me out the back way.

I climbed into her red pick-up truck. She started the engine then turned it off. She proceeded to explain to me that we had shared "the pipe" and that this meant she trusted and loved me. Marla further explained that this was even more binding than if I had sworn on a bible. I told her that I wasn't sure I believed in God. She got pissed and told me that I had better get right with Jesus. I started to laugh thinking that she was teasing me but I quickly realized that she was dead serious.

She lit a cigarette and told me that she would have to hurt me or have Jerry hurt me if I ever even thought about cheating them or turning them in. I was actually quite hurt. I told her that I could never narc on them. I loved them and my

job. I told her that I thought she was the coolest person I had ever known. Marla seemed pleased. She told me I was a smart kid. She added a comment that I also had, from what she had heard, a pretty big dick. I blushed. This made her giggle more. She reached over and messed my hair telling me that I should be pleased when anyone told me that I had a big dick.

She started up the truck and we were on our way. She already knew how to get to my house, which surprised me. She said something about having my number and all the numbers of the people who worked for she and Jerry.

She asked me if I wanted to have Jerry teach me how to make the donuts during my summer break. I was thrilled. I don't think I had ever felt so cool in my life. Of course, it would be a couple of weeks before I found out that this meant I had to be at work by four o'clock in the morning. Turned out that Jerry was quite serious about making the donuts.

We pulled into the driveway of my parents' house.

"Bummer of a house, kid."

"Yeah."

"Here. This is for you. Share it with someone you love or sell it. Make some money."

She had handed me a fairly large bag of weed. I stuffed it into my pants, leaned over and gave her a kiss on the cheek. She smiled.

I got down from the truck. I sort of stumbled into the house and avoided my mother who called from the dining room. I could hear my little brother screaming and my father demanding that she shut him up.

I closed myself in my room, hid the bag under the mattress of my waterbed, turned on the record player and

jumped into bed. I was floating as I closed my eyes and Patti Smith began to sing about the land of a thousand dances. I fell asleep and dreamed of Marla, Jerry and Clifford all fucking on the glaze table.

When I woke up, the sheets were wet.

BONDING WITH JUNKIES

At the age of 18, the medication was prescribed...

...as a "deal" established with a doctor. I agreed to stop taking Valium as well as smoking weed and my beloved

cigarettes. I didn't exactly hold true on that deal, but the prescribed medication has remained, even now, well into the end of my thirties. The dosage has become so low, it really doesn't do anything anymore. But my body is used to having it in its system, so I must take it or risk serious side effects. I could go off it, but that takes doctor supervision and about 6 months of cutting already small tablets into even smaller pieces. A pain. So, over the years, I delay going off a drug that I no longer need.

Without insurance this little drug is so expensive I have to turn to government assistance. Insurance coverage is still a few months away...so it is off to the free clinic. Lucky to have access to such a service, but it takes an entire Saturday. Still, one can't beat the interesting interactions one encounters at a San Francisco city clinic in the Western Addition.

"Hey, baby! I haven't seen your tiny ass in here for months! How you doin' baby-child?"

"Sharonda! Good to see you!"

A hug is exchanged.

"I'm cool. Am in between insurance and had to get my dolls refilled. Same old same old. How are you?"

"Oh, you know. Still tryin' to get my shit together. Woke up this mornin' in some low down piece of shit hotel room and just look at my arm!"

She rolls up sleeves of her frilly top to reveal puss filled track marks which emit a sort of sour smell. I fight the urge to recoil.

"Oh, sweetie! Are you cleaning your works? And, why are you still shooting into your arms?"

"Oh, Matty. I am sorry, but I can't be shooting under my

tongue! That shit hurts like a son-of-a-bitch!"

"No! Sharonda! Shoot up behind your knee so your arms can heal!"

"Oh, baby these arms are scarred for life and I'm usually too tired to do all that aerobics shit to shoot my stuff."

"Hey! You two! Let's stop talking about where to shoot up and talk about how to stop shooting up!"

(I guess I pissed off the front desk guy again.)

"Oh, shut the fuck up! When am I gonna see the doctor?! My arm is killin' me!"

I lean past Sharonda and ask Joe if he's even looked at her arm. "Joe, it looks like she's badly infected. Can't you guys get her in quicker?"

"*Thank you!*" Sharonda turns her head toward Joe as if waiting for an apology. Joe gets up and walks over to us. She holds out her arm for him to inspect.

"Oh, man. Okay. We need to get you to the hospital. We told you that there's an infection going around. This looks like botulism. Are you having any odd symptoms?"

"I told you people I came in 'cuz this shit hurts, stinks and 'm having trouble seeing. You're all blurry...which is just as good 'cuz you is one *ugly* muthafucka!"

Joe rolls his eyes. "Hold on." He walks away. It is just Sharonda, me and some guy asleep in the chair under the TV.

"What in the *fuck* is botulism?"

That's when I noticed the blue signs on all the walls warning *H* users about an infection that is spreading among

users in SF. Heroin botulism which, according to the blue signs can be fatal if not treated.

"I think it just means you have an infection. But it can be serious so you need to do whatever they tell you do to. Okay? I mean, you really need to try to quit."

"I know. And, honey, you need to get a job with insurance so you don't have to bring yo pretty white ass in here anymore...'r do you like chillin' out with us freaks?"

"I love chillin' out with you Sharonda!"

She laughs. "Pay up then!" She extends her hand. I laugh. She sighs and rubs her sleeve. I can't decide if it's bleeding, but something is leaking through the material of her sleeve. I couldn't help it, I am sure I sort of recoiled. Gross.

Joe and this cute young doctor walk out. The doctor can't be more than about 24 years old and she looks like she just stepped off the bus from Idaho. She is wearing latex gloves.

She smiles at Sharonda as if smiling at a small puppy, "Hi. Let's see that arm of yours!"

"Shit. Are we gonna have a party, bitch?"

I fight the urge to laugh. It really isn't at all funny, but what can one do? Joe tells Sharonda to shut up.

One of the counselors comes out. They explain to Sharonda that he is going to drive her to the city hospital and that she needs to be treated as soon as possible.

"Shit. OK."

She gathers up her stuff, motions for me to stand up and give her a hug. I do. "Take care of yourself. OK?"

"Yeah, yeah. I'll see you later!" And, with that Sharonda and the counselor walk out into the sunshine.

Joe and the cute little doctor walk down the hall. I hear her ask Joe if Sharonda is a woman or a 'transgender.' In a hushed tone, I hear him say that she is a *tranny*.

I sit and think about their hushed conversation.

Why does it matter? And isn't she a 'woman' according to *their* standards? I mean, to everyone else she is a 'woman.' To her, she is a 'woman.' Why does it matter? Will she be okay? And, if she is okay will she just continue on and get sick again?

I look around the room at all the blue, red, green, white and yellow "Alert!" and "Warning!" signs transcribed in several languages.

A kid walks in.

He is handsome, but smells bad. He can't read to fill out his forms, so Joe helps him. I hear Joe ask the kid where he is living. The kid gives the name of some shelter in the Mission District. Joe asks him how long he has been in San Francisco. The kid doesn't know. He thinks "maybe a year or two."

He volunteers that he came to the city from Nebraska to be in a band. When asked his education level, the kid tells Joe that he "finished 9th grade." The *kid* is actually 29 years old. He sits next to me, but doesn't say anything.

A few minutes pass.

I hear my name called. The cute doctor is ready to see me. As I follow her down the hall she tells me it is a relief to see someone who has it together and just needs some temporary assistance. Our conversation is professional but friendly. She is new to San Francisco and to this job. Ten minutes later, I am back in the sunshine. Blondie is on the iPod and I'm headed to

Walgreens to pick up my government prescriptions.

As I walk down the street that I would never dream of walking after sunset, I think to myself, "How in the hell did I get here? Life is such a trip."

CONFESSIONS FROM A TUBE SOCK
...CIRCA 1979

As I am want to do...

...while engaging in conversations with my friends, I pursued a better understanding of us all by asking when we

each discovered the magical powers of masturbation. Being my friends, no one was at all ashamed or afraid to discuss in detail. So, it was very interesting.

I discovered that I was a bit late in the game of sexual discovery when compared to my friends. I can remember when my *Gay Little Heart* found its way to an erection watching Kris Kristofferson romp about *sans* clothes with Barbra Streisand in A STAR IS BORN. I was a little kid. I was frightened and had to ask for an explanation from my cool 70's mom, who was at my side watching the film in the sold out Gaylin Theater.

However, it would end up being several years before I discovered to where an erection could lead. For me, I was about thirteen years old. I was in the tub reading "Rolling Stone." I can remember spending more time than required looking at the cover shot of Robin Williams. I remember being worried that I was getting the newsprint wet as I am old enough to remember when "Rolling Stone" was in newspaper format.

I placed the magazine down on the yellow tile floor next to the tub. Yes, I had an erection. By this time, I thought nothing of it. I was not ashamed or embarrassed. But I knew to be discreet. My mother was quite sex positive...until she decided to go through a 'born again' phase which lasted a horrible five years. That, however, is a whole other story...and decade. This was 1979 and Mom was still listening to Elton John.

As for discovery of the Big O, I had to raise up on my knees to reach the soap. Ivory soap, I might add. As I reached up for the soap, the hot water poured down upon my unsuspecting member. The gush of hot water created a favorable *sin-sa-tion*. I remember staying fixed with the water running full force on my enlarged organ. I remember turning to my left and glancing down at Mork on the cover of The Rolling Stone. Who knew someone from a planet called Ork could ever be so appealing?

I will never forget the feeling that took me over. My thighs felt like they were giving 'way. I had to turn away from the lovely picture and hold my palms out in front of me against the tiles. I came.

I fell back into the water sending a wave of soapy water over the tub and on to the floor and fully drenching the magazine, which had led me to such pleasure. Pleasure. I was also quite frightened. I remember thinking that I must have somehow gotten soap inside me. What was that stuff that had just spurt out of me?

This brought me to another conversation with my mother. Luckily, she didn't use any of the posters on my wall as visual pointers and I did not tell her of the Robin Williams picture. She seemed to be fairly sure I was gay anyway.

For years she blamed Barbra Streisand. Granted. It was odd for a four year old to become obsessed with Barbra Streisand, but I am fairly sure she had nothing to do with my being queer.

Mom felt I played *The Wet* LP way more than was necessary. Oh well. I think she still might blame Babs for my being gay. Anyway, she explained that the stuff was sperm and all normal. Actually, she had explained sex to me over and over again. I think she was a bit annoyed. I remember her pinning up her hair as if she was getting ready for a swim.

"You came. That's all. No big deal. I've got to get going" and with that she picked up my baby brother and tailed it to the pool. At that time, she had begun to passively flirt with this hairy guy who owned a local record store. Sadly, she never followed through and ended up re-married to my nightmare of a father. But, once again, that is a whole different story.

Within a few months I had discovered the pleasures that could be added with the aid of my grandmother's Vaseline.

I spent a lot of time with Grandmother in Houston. I would hang out at her pool and watch her hot gay neighbors swim in the apartment complex pool. One was a hair stylist and the other was about to become a doctor. The stylist had hair just like John Travolta from the BOY IN THE PLASTIC BUBBLE days and his lover had his hair styled really short like a new wave singer. I would not go swimming with them because they rather excited the thirteen year old in me. I think they knew.

I remember both of them asking me about the movies and music I liked. The *punk-looking-soon-to-be-doctor* attempted to explain that Elton John's 'Tiny Dancer' was actually about Elton's penis. It was only recently that I realized what he was talking about. I kept trying to steer the conversation away from all things gay to other topics of interest like weed, Pink Floyd, The Who and Led Zeppelin (all of which I had become a bit of an expert). But, they only wanted to pry into me about being possibly queer.

"Matty, have you heard the 12" version of 'No More Tears'?"

"Do you like Ted's wife beater? Do you want one?"

"Come on in and swim!"

"Did you want to cry at the end of A STAR IS BORN?"

My answer to these questions was really "yes" but I always said "no" before giving myself away.

One of them asked me if I liked to play with my tube sock.

I was wearing my blue gym shorts with matching tube socks. When I asked what he meant, they both laughed. My Grandmother was inside baking cookies. The stylist told me that he liked to jerk off into his gym socks.

"Jerk off?"

"Oh, you know! Masturbate!"

I could feel my face flush, but about three minutes later, filled with thoughts of my Grandmother's gay neighbors in their tiny jean cut-offs, I was locked in my Grandmother's powder blue bathroom. Spread out on my back on her blue carpet, my feet pushed against her blue toilet and my head jammed against the blue door. I scooped out a large portion of her Vaseline and inserted into one of my tube socks. I slid the sock over my cock. I closed my eyes. Moved my hand around my sock with wild abandon. My thighs and knees gave out a lot that summer of 1979.

Just me, my tube sock, a glob of Vaseline, a blue bathroom and my head filled with erotic thoughts. Oh, the joys of self-discovery!

Sure, over the course of the years I've done my share of exploration and continue to do so. But there is something magical about discovering what joys can come from within and spring from the mind.

God bless Robin Williams and my grandmother's gay neighbors, wherever they all might be.

PHONE SEX BOY

I have told very few people about this experience....

I am not sure why. I am not ashamed of it. But people can cast judgments or project ideas onto you that have no validity.

But, it's raining and I now find myself sitting in a certain café. I once visited this café after a one-night stand...a desperate one-night stand that was really an attempt to silence loneliness shortly after I had returned to San Francisco from Boston. In all fairness, I didn't know it was to be a one-night stand until the event was over. In less than a few minutes after the deed was done, I was walking toward a bus stop feeling sad. Before I arrived at the MUNI bus stop, I ended up in what I like to call *The Sad Café*. And now, I am experiencing this café during a sunny afternoon.

As I sit here reviewing that dreary experience that we all know a bit too well, a time in my life came to mind. In the spirit of my new life and my commitment to being true to myself, it might be cool to actually write about it. I think what amuses me the most is that it really means nothing. It was just an excursion of youth taken out of desperation for food money.

And in the spring of 1991, I was desperate. The temp work I was getting was not paying enough to make rent *and* eat. I was discovering that my hard-earned degree in English was worth less than the parchment paper upon which it was printed. My job search was going nowhere. How many times did I hear, "Why aren't you teaching?"...and I was so very tired of only one meal a day. I should add that that meal was always Ramen Noodles out of a small bag.

So, I was lying in my sleeping bag with Patti Smith booming from my CD player reading *Bay Windows*, the Boston weekly gay rag. I came across a plain text ad for adult phone sex work and no experience was required. I called the number. The next evening, after I left my temp post I headed over to a tiny office near the Boston Common.

It was on the 4th floor. The office was tiny and smelled of stale coffee and incense. I walked in and discovered a set of cubes and two fairly rough looking lesbians. Actually, they both

would have called themselves 'dykes.' One of them was wearing a *wife-beater* that read "Bull Dyke" across the chest. Her name was Bea and she was in charge. But, her skinny girlfriend, Jo wrote the checks.

There were three things on the walls:

 * A poster of Joan Crawford holding a rifle in a manly western gear. This was a still from JOHNNY GUITAR and I wanted it!
 * Another poster of Nirvana's promoting their classic "Bleach" album and I wanted that as well.
 * A blow up of an ad for phone sex that had a picture of a girl in bikini that I didn't want.

This last hanging work of art was the first ad that Bea and her girlfriend had ever posted. This was still a new enterprise for them. And now, they wanted to offer the same service to gay/bi callers. That is where the Bay Windows help wanted bit came into play.

They were looking to hire five guys.

I was asked if I could be available from 9 PM to 2 AM, three times a week.

I cringed. I didn't like the idea of walking home from this part of the city that late. Jo explained that I would only be coming to the office to pick up my pay if I got the job. They didn't want any flakes or drug addicts. Bea told me that I sounded cute and responsible on the phone and that was why I was there.

I had to audition.

There was a cluster of four small office cubicles which sort of formed a makeshift office. Bea had me go to the cube opposite she and Jo. I could only see the top of their heads.

Jo had handed me an odd looking mobile phone...big and clunky. It had the look of a walkie-talkie, circa WWI.

It beeped.

One of them was calling me.

Bea: "OK, connecting Mr. Jones. He wants to talk to a high school student. He is your principal and has found a fag magazine in your locker. Your name is Bobby. He is into rough talk and rough sex. Here he is."

Jo: "Hello?"

"Mr. Jones? This is Bobby. I am really embarrassed. I'll do anything, but please don't tell my Dad. He will kill me if he finds out I'm gay!"

Jo: "Bobby, I have to tell him. You brought your cocksucker pornography into the school. I can't have that. How do you think this makes me feel?"

"But, Mr. Jones, I will do anything! Just please don't tell my parents!"

Jo: "Well, Bobby. What can you do to make me reconsider?"

"*Anything* you want, *but please don't hurt me*, `kay?"

"Oh, I think some punishment is in order. Come on. What are you going to do for me?"

"Something that you'll like. I don't want you to hurt me, but I noticed a nightstick in the locker room. I kinda like nightsticks, you know?"

"Tough. I'm going to hurt you. Now, this nightstick... Tell me what I can do to you that might put my mind at ease about

not talking to your parents."

I won't take this any further, but my ideas involving a nightstick worked well for Jo and Bea. I then took more calls from them. I was there for about an hour. I knew the goal was to keep the person on the phone for as long as I could and to say things that person would want to hear. Bea would prompt me before Jo got on the phone and took on another scenario. I did the student/punishment conversations several times. I did a couple of fucked-up daddy/son chats. I did a tick/slut discussion once. I scored high marks on these.

However, I didn't do great as the coach, the teacher, the dad or the punisher. But, this turned out to be cool. I guess the other guys that they had met were older and Bea felt they had the 'top' side covered. She felt that they needed some young, submissive bottom types. Jo agreed.

I got the job.

I was 'loaned' one of these giant mobile phones. I don't have my journal with me, but I believe my nights were Tuesdays, Wednesdays and Thursdays. I have to admit, I kind of enjoyed it for the first couple of weeks. I thought it was funny and it was kind of cool to be able to see how long I was able keep a guy on the phone. I also thought it was endlessly interesting to hear and discover what turned people on. It was so difficult to not discuss this adventure with my friends, but I never mentioned it.

During my first month as a *phone sex boy*, I thought I had it made! The extra money was great! It wasn't that much. I got $30 a night. If I kept someone on the phone for more than 30 minutes, I got an extra $10 for each of those calls. And it was all paid to me in cash. It was safe, easy, kept me eating and allowed me to see a movie a week.

The most interesting 'conversations' I had were with straight women. I still don't get this. But, sometimes I would

get a call from women who wanted to talk to a gay guy who would explain everything he liked to do in graphic detail. I would be told what aspect of gay sex was of interest and go from there. I guess this happened about ten times. And a couple of the women would masturbate as I talked to and with them. I wanted so badly to ask what it was about hearing a gay guy describe hot gay sex that got them off.

I *still* wonder about that. I would not find it erotic to sit and listen to a woman walk me through what she likes to do or have done to her by a man or another woman. I would find it interesting...but not erotic or arousing. But, then again, phone sex doesn't interest me that much at all. Which might be why I started hating it so much.

Only one call ever disturbed me. I got this guy who wanted to hurt me in his fantasy discussion. So, he started telling me what he was doing to me and it got violent. His fantasy reached the point where he was slicing me with a knife. By this point, I just stopped talking. He kept going. After a few minutes of total silence from my end, he stopped.

Silence.

Then, back into a normal voice he asked, "Hey, are you there?" I remember not being sure of what to do. Before I could stop myself I said, "I think you hit an artery. You killed me, dude." I was playing a skater. He hung up.

When I would stop by the office every Friday to pick up my money, I would sometimes meet other operators. It was interesting because it seemed that all of the women were lesbian, large and older. There was one lady who could not be a day under 60. But I gathered she was their best. I seemed to run into her every Friday. I only ever met one of the other four guys. He was physically challenged and had the look of a librarian. Interesting.

By the second month, I was flipping through magazines as

I chatted with the callers and sometimes watching videos without sound. VALLEY OF THE DOLLS was my favorite. Often, I found that I had the desire to clean the apartment while chatting...but the phone was too heavy.

The calls I got were fairly 'normal' sex fantasies revolving around a younger guy getting punished by his father or teacher. This was 'my' standard caller. What was funny at first became dull and gross in the end.

I can still remember feeling more than a little scared as I walked off the elevator to return the phone. Jo didn't seem surprised. Bea asked me if I would reconsider.

I said no.

Jo inspected my phone and then gave me my money. The disabled librarian-looking guy was there. I ended up taking the elevator down with the disabled librarian-looking phone sex boy.

As I held the door open for him, he told me that Bea had told him I was her best male operator.

GIANT SPIDERS

It wasn't so much the loud bang...

The pieces of sheet rock that landed on my head or even the gun aimed just above my head didn't frighten me as much

47

as the smell. I guess it was a mixture of gun powder and the particles from the wall. I remember thinking it smelled of a cannon having been fired above my head. In retrospect, I don't understand why no one did anything about my father's behavior. I think we tossed it off as eccentricity and, at that time, whiskey.

My mother came running into the room. I was shaking the white powder and bits out of my bowl haircut. Dad sitting across from me, whiskey glass in his left hand and .45 mag in his right still aimed just a bit above my head. My mother was in her blue shorts and patchwork button-up shirt, her thin arms flat against her sides. "What in the hell are you doing to the walls? And put that goddamn gun down! Are you fucking crazy?"

Never one to sit quietly and a smart-ass at seven, I answered her last question, "Yeah. He's crazy!"

"Shut up! Don't talk like that!"

Dad just sat there looking confused.

The gun was now resting on his knee, but I remember thinking that this was even worse because now it was aimed right at me. I remember wondering what it might feel like if he shot and the bullet splattered into my chest. How bad would it hurt? Would it hurt more than other things that had started to happen? But, I would start to get dizzy when I thought about such things.

So, I began to hum.

"What were you doing? Do you realize how close that was to your son? He's a little boy!" At this point mom began to run her long fingers through my hair and teasing the plaster crap on to the floor. "Go to your room" she directed.

"No."

I just sit there humming staring across at the barrel of the pistol that was pointed at me.

"Pat, give me the gun!" My mother seemed calm.

Dad sort of zoned back in and shook his head to indicate that he would not relinquish the gun to her or anyone. He finished off his whiskey and glared at me. I wasn't scared. I glared back at him. I remember thinking how much trouble he would get into if he did shoot me.

"What were you doing?" Mom was not going to let him off.

He sighed and just let the glass drop to the floor. It didn't break. It just rolled across toward us and under the couch.

"I was trying to protect our son! I saw another one of those giant spiders crawling down the wall! It was going for him! I didn't want that fucking spider to bite him. So, I just shot the fucker. He's lying behind the couch on the floor dead. I fucking saved your son!"

Giant spiders. This was a relatively new thing. He had been *seeing* giant spiders a lot. Even reality, normal life spiders terrified him. Six feet tall, always in a cowboy hat, boots and way too heavy...I always found it amusing that a little insect could cause him so much fear. Instead of being ashamed of this fear, he would joke about it. It just added to some form of *mystique* that he might have been trying to create.

My father was fat. But he somehow carried it in a way that didn't seem so pathetic. It seemed a bit menacing and women flirted with him all the time. My mom was hot. My dad's friends watched her a lot. And, I think she liked the attention. And hated it all at once.

But now, the giant spiders were coming for me.

I could hear my Grandmother knocking at the door that separated her little house from ours. I wanted to go, open the door and let her take me into her house. But, I knew that would be a mistake.

"We're fine!"

But, grandmother was not going to listen to my mom. She never did. She just kept knocking. I don't think they ever gave her the key to our part of the house.

"So, you saw more of these giant spiders. How much have you had to drink?"

"Not enough. Shut the fuck up with the humming! You sound like a fucking girl!"

Dad's attempt at humiliation only made me want to stop with the humming and start singing full on. But, I knew that would be dumb. I stopped humming.

"I am so sick of your shit! I will not have you shooting guns in the house and you will not shoot them that close to him!"

Dad stood up. His gun fell back into his recliner. He was heading for her. She could move quick. Despite her small frame, she was able to pick me up in one swoop. My head was pressed into her breasts. She smelled like that faux French perfume she kept on her dresser.

As he sort of fell toward us, she managed to move us to the side of his recliner. But, I don't think he was going to hit her because he simply pulled the couch several feet from what was left of the wall.

"I want the two of you to look at this dead motherfucker!"

Grandmother's knocking was getting really loud and I could hear my mentally-challenged uncle calling my dad's name. His odd voice sounding even more child like than usual.

I remember everything sort of freezing for a minute. Dad stood there staring down at the space between the wall and the couch. I guess he couldn't find the dead giant spider. He let out a stream of curse words and punched a hole through the wall.

"We're leaving."

And, with that Mom carried me out the front door. She didn't have to tell me what to do. I crawled into her blue Volkswagen Bug and plunged myself into the passenger seat. She jumped in and slammed the door. I could hear him calling her name. I don't think she bothered to look behind us. She pushed the pedal down, moved the car into gear and we backed out of the yard at a high speed. We were soon speeding down the street.

A couple of neighbors were outside watching. I felt embarrassed. She never seemed to notice the stares. Actually, she seldom took notice of the neighbors. But, they were watching. My mother never seemed to notice much of anything...or, such was my perception.

She was crying and that always made me feel bad.

I plugged her tape in. Elton John was singing about *electric boots* and *mohair'd suits*. I started singing at the top of my lungs. She started laughing. We drove and drove. At one point, she slammed on the brakes, shut the 8-track tape player off and looked at me. The make-up around her eyes was all funny looking. She looked like a sparkling raccoon. I loved that tan stuff with glitter she rubbed into her skin, but her hair was all messy, like she had forgotten to use her hairspray or something.

"Baby, has Daddy been touching you in ways that are wrong? Has Daddy tried to hurt you? Mommy needs you to tell her."

I stared ahead. Was that a horn honking at us? I wondered if she would take me to a movie or drop me off at the movies for a while.

"Baby?"

"No."

She was crying again, but we were moving.

She pulled the little car into a parking lot in front of the parking lot of a strip mall where we sometimes watched fireworks. I wasn't sure, but I thought that there was a movie theater near us. I so wanted to go to a movie. I thought about jumping out of the car and trying to find it.

I wanted to just run away. I just wanted to get away.

She pushed the tape back in and turned the volume up high. She was punching the buttons and found the track about Benny and the Jets that we both loved. The lights in the parking lot had come on. It was dark. I wondered how late it was.

"C'mon! Let's dance!"

Mom got out of the car. I tried to get the passenger door to open, but it wouldn't budge. So, I crawled over the stick shift and got out of the car. I hated my shorts. They were plaid. Grandmother had made them for me so I felt like I had to wear them. I liked the way the pavement felt on my feet. She took my hands and we started dancing to Elton John. She was singing along like me. She picked me up and twirled me around.

We were both singing and laughing. A van of older boys drove by and called out things to us that I knew were aimed at my mom. She both hated and loved that sort of attention. They parked their van a little ways away from us and were watching us. I felt a little scared, but she had no fear. She was lost in the music.

And, I think, for a few minutes...my mother was happy.

LILY AND ANOTHER BEAUTIFUL DAY

I no longer have to ask for what I want...

Cindy, behind the counter was pulling my order all together as I walked toward her. But, something was in the air today

that made the atmosphere feel somehow different.

There was an interesting lady at the counter ahead of me. She looked like a ballet dancer gone to seed. I would guess she was in her mid to late fifties and painfully thin. Hair twisted in a tight bun and dressed in thrift-shop chic. However, it was clear she had money. While her skirt, shirt and sweater were most certainly designer vintage, her shoes were not. Spiked heeled to the point of fetish and little black ribbons that ran and tied up her calves. Wearing red silk stockings and a few very expensive diamond rings, this woman was quite busy working a sort of classy/sleaze/slut look.

The problem was her face. Not enough make-up to match this look she was attempting to create. And, the pains of time and too many miles traced their way across her cheeks and around her deep sunken eyes. She had the appearance of fragility, tiredness and the sort of exhaustion that teeters dangerously on the edge of anger.

One could immediately see that Cindy had her fill of this interesting woman. Normally happy-go-lucky and free with her spirit, Cindy was clearly not happy. This interesting woman, this customer, had been at the counter for more than a few minutes. As I watched, I decided to name her. To me, there seemed to be no other name that could come close to capturing what I saw other than this name: Lily. As far as I was concerned this was Lily and she was having some issues despite the beauty of the weather.

Lily stood with her right foot extended so far I thought she might break out in dance at any moment. Her left hand, decorated with long red fingernails was placed firmly on the top of the counter. Lily's right hand was touching the side of her face as if she were trying to solve life's ultimate mystery and she was sighing.

"Well, they all look divine, but how can you not sell sugar-free pastry?" Lily stood poised waiting for Cindy to respond.

Cindy seemed to be grounded in opposition and provided no response. This was a most unusual action for such a person as Cindy.

"I just don't know what I want. I'm sorry, but there is both so very much and yet so very little."

"Well, here is your tea. Why don't I ring that up and assist my other customer?"

Lily turned and looked at me. I looked at Lily. Lily frowned and I smiled. A moment of confusion flashed across her face. She quickly returned her attention to the pastries, which were waiting under the glass. Lily was on a mission and this was her turn.

"I guess the croissant has the least sugar, but each one probably has a stick of butter. Is that correct?"

Again, no response was given. Cindy was in no mood.

"And, you say that these ring shaped things are more sugar-like than bread orientation?"

Cindy shot me a look that screamed, 'I'm going kill this white ass bitch!' but she did not. No. After shooting me this look, Cindy simply turned those frustrated eyes back to Lily.

"Well, I need to think a bit more. Why don't you help this young man?" And, with that, Lily turned and watched Cindy and me with more scrutiny than she had given the pastries. I got my cookie and Diet Coke.

"Excuse me, but do you have any idea how much sugar is in that huge cookie?" Lily was speaking to me.

"A lot I should think. You see, this is a pastry shop and this is a chocolate chip cookie." I did my very best Vanna White

and modeled my cookie to Lily. Cindy laughed out loud enjoying the moment.

"Well, you appear to be in good shape so you must know what you're doing. I like your jacket. Is it Diesel?" Lily's right hand gently stroked my jacket that I had only the day before found at the thrift shop for $15. It *was* Diesel.

"Look lady, leave my customer alone. You either order something, pay for your tea or leave my store." Cindy was beyond pissed.

"I'll take an oatmeal cookie, but I would like to see more healthy options in the future!"

Fast forward about an hour... Two middle-aged men enter the café. Each of these men was holding the hands of two little girls. I guessed these two guys to be in their mid-forties. They were wearing coordinated tracksuits. One was orange and the other was blue. It was a Howard Johnson's kind of moment, except they were both gayer than one could even imagine. It didn't take long to know that the two little girls were their adopted daughters.

The domestic partner in orange was tall and thin. The other domestic partner in blue was not so tall and a bit chubby. The two girls looked like they could be twins. One wore a dress and the other was dressed in a little jumper outfit. These little girls could not have been any older than six years of age.

"Honey, why don't you take care of Kayla and I will take care of Kara."

"Okay."

The girls were hyperactive and it was not long before they began to upset Lily who had been sipping her tea, playing with her cookie and staring off into space ever since she sat down. However, these very noisy children had interrupted Lily and I

doubt that children ever acted this way in her presence.

The gay fathers were oblivious to the fact that their daughters' collective voices rivaled a sonic boom. Cindy was becoming distressed. It was impossible to understand what either child wanted. The odd thing was that the two daddies seemed to be amused and enjoyed the chaos.

And, as if on cue, a very flamboyant pair of boys entered. Each Castro Boy wore tight jeans and mesh power tank tops despite the cool weather. Despite their Olympic Weight Lifter bodies, they had the voices of teenage girls. These two boys were walking stereotypes just waiting for a Gay Pride Parade.

It only took a moment before they were both horrified by the noisy children and the ugly track suited gay fathers.

Lily just could not and would not take it for even a moment longer. Sitting down her cup of tea and turning her attention to the two fathers, her voice hit a register I had not thought possible.

"Please shut your fucking brats up! This is not a zoo! Some of us are trying to think!!"

Lily found an eager fan base with the two Castro Boys who immediately screamed out, "You go, Miss Thang!"

The little girls shut up. Orange Tracksuited Gay Father looked quite angry, but Blue Track Suited Father looked worried. Four cookies were quickly ordered and the noise of the tracksuits and the little girls vanished with the slam of the door. The Castro Boys wanted a ten-dollar bill broken. Well, that wasn't going to happen. Annoyed and pissed off they virtually flew out of the café.

I looked over at Lily. And, despite the perfect day waiting outside, her face was filled with a sadness that refused to be hidden.

QUIET RIOT

I wanted to write something of interest...

...but being drugged since Thursday has not done much for my creative juices. I was going to write about my fancy new

dental bleaching trays which are meant to brighten my teeth up by 4 shades and how the bleaching material manages to make my teeth even more sensitive to air, water and life in general. However, I fear that this would be dull and too self-indulgent.

So, instead, I am transcribing the last little story I ever wrote about my life, which I have retained. Actually, I do not think I have ever shared this one with anyone. So, this little document, which I wrote about three years ago, comes to you like a virgin kissed for the very first time. I recently discussed this with my brother thinking he never knew about any of it. He told me that I had related these and other driving adventures to him on several occasions. I guess I was wrong.

I applied and was approved for a Texas Hardship Driving License. This was something that Texas used to allow. I had to work and needed to help my mom pick up my baby brother from day care. My father had acquired a car for me after a neighbor's husband had killed himself in the back seat. It was ugly as hell. A 1966 Buick Special Deluxe in lovely green. It would probably be worth a small fortune now, but to a kid in the 1980's it was a nightmare of a car.

I used to joke that if one leaned on the car, he or she would suffer a nasty cut as this car had razor sharp Batman Car-like angles that should only ever be imposed in science fiction. It was almost impossible to navigate into parking spaces. Also, no matter how hard I cleaned/scrubbed, I was never able to get the blood stains off the fabric lined roof. Apparently, the police do not clean up after someone blows his brains out in the back seat of the family car. This was the primary motive for our neighbor to sell the car to my father for fifty dollars. Or, so he told me.

"It's a classic! Stop being a fag and clean it! Most boys would be thrilled to have their own car!" And, my parents did somehow buy me a cool stereo cassette system for the automobile!

60

My friends liked to call this car the *Shit-mobile*. I preferred *Matt-mobile* but that never stuck. Most tried to avoid the back seat if I actually took the time to explain those odd stains. Except my friends, Betty and Karla, who seemed oddly drawn to the back seat due to this backstory. My kind of girls!

My brother had two car seats. One was usually to be found attached in my back seat on the passenger side of my Buick. This was so I could see him in my rear view mirror as I drove. I love my brother and may be a biased, but I think he was the cutest baby ever. My friend Lisha and I used to take him to the mall so that people would think he was our child. This was Texas in the early 80's. It really would not have been that unusual for a couple of teens to have a kid. Though, I think she and I were about fourteen.

Roy was a cute toddler. He was also a bit of a demon-child for several years. My friends were just so happy that I had a car that everyone agreed to help me watch him so we could speed about the city. I was only to drive at certain times and these would normally be the times that he was with me. My friends and I also enjoyed the many horror stories of Roy Temper Tantrums.

Looking back, it is a miracle I never wrecked. My baby brother joined in many a misadventure and added either much fun or much pain depending upon his mood. We did enjoy it when he would just lose it as we ordered into one of those drive-thru speaker boxes and the poor window clerk could hear nothing but stoned kids and a crying baby. And, Roy knew how to cry at volumes far louder than any car stereo could beat. If my tape player was cranked to '10,' Roy was cranked to '11.' Roy was not to be outdone by some lame music. No. He would never allow that.

At times I would try to emote paternal. This was usually a bad choice on my part because I had horrible luck with these sorts of actions. A good example was when Roy joined me as I

drove a friend off to the far edges of our county. I was taking this pal to a dealer's house. Scratch that. This is not a good example of my paternal streak. However, after leaving my friend to further his addiction, it was just me and my brother driving down an old country road. I was driving slowly because this was a dirt road filled with potholes and if the ride got too bumpy he would start crying.

A cute little rabbit ran out a short ways in front of the car. My paternal instinct kicked in.

"Roy! Look behind us! A bunny rabbit! Do you think it's the Easter Bunny? Look!" as I stopped the car.

Roy was screaming in horror before I could turn around. Yes. I had not only struck the rabbit. It had sort of broken into a bloody mess as my back tire rolled over the once cute creature. I had to climb into the back seat and comfort him. I did my best to convince him that the bloody pulp behind us was not ever a living animal. I felt so bad. I guess the potholes had numbed me and I had not felt the bump of a tiny rabbit. So, to my three-year-old brother, I had just killed the Easter Bunny. Terrible.

However, the worst incident happened later that summer. Siouxsie and The Banshees' *Scream* cassette was blaring from my tape player as Roy and I whizzed down the road. We had just been to the mall. This was 1982 and I had just picked up a way cool shirt from Chess King. Roy was tired from the trip and had fallen asleep.

All four windows were down. The wind was blowing and I was feeling great. I did my best to keep my cigarette low as to not blow too much smoke or ash to the back seat. This was a lone road and I felt like I owned it. Now, as ugly as it was, my Buick could go fast. I was edging past 80 MPH as Siouxsie and I sang to the top of our lungs. I thought I noted something flying right at my head. I remember thinking, "Oh wow! Is that a bird?"

It was. And this particular bird managed to fly right into the side panel of the driver's window. Now, I guess a number of things can happen when a small bird flies into the side panel of a car window when the car is going about 80 MPH and that bird is flying full force. On this particular occasion, the result was that the little bird bounced into the car and slammed against the interior of the back window. At some point during the bounce into my car, the head of the bird snapped off. It all happened so quickly.

I tried to remain calm. I put my cig in the ashtray, turned off the music, slowed down and watched in the mirror as feathers flew all around us. Blood streamed down the inside of my back window and the bird sort of flapped about on the back board beneath the glass...directly behind the head of my sleeping baby brother.

"Oh God. Please don't let the headless body flap on to the toddler's head!"

I stopped the car. I waved the feathers away from my face. I waited for my brother to start screaming in trauma. But there was no sound from the back seat other than a sort of manic flapping/thud sound which stopped soon enough.

Silence.

I picked up my cigarette and took a long, deep drag. I picked up my Sonic cup and took a sip of soda.

It had to be done. I turned around to check on Roy.

There he sat. Sleeping soundly, covered in blood and feathers. And, a bird head seated in the tray of his baby seat by his half eaten cookie. Luckily, the body of the bird lay behind his head.

"Just drive slowly. Just one more mile or so and we're

home. I can get him out of the car and he never needs to know."

My brother could be a fairly sound sleeper. I can't drive or do much of anything without music. However, at that time, some music was more soothing to Roy than others. Led Zep/ The Who used to kind of freak him out. Blondie and Fleetwood Mac made him hyper. Goth rock didn't bother him too much either way but could still be a risk. But, much to his embarrassment now, Barbra Streisand would often lull him into slumber. So, I quickly slipped in *Lazy Afternoon* and proceeded to drive home at a very slow speed. As I pulled into the driveway, I was so very relieved to discover that he was still sound asleep.

I left Barbra singing about letters that cross in the mail or some such and ran into the house where I grabbed a bottle of those wet napkins with which I was always dousing Roy, a bottle of Windex, a roll of paper towels and the kitchen garbage can. I climbed into the back seat and began to softly pull the feathers off my baby brother. The feathers had already started to jell into the blood that had also splattered. Roy was sticky with bird gore and feathered. This was summer in southeast Texas. My brother was also sweating. I was doing my best to gently wipe his forehead and face to prevent any bird blood from slipping on top of his eyelids.

Roy started to stir.

Shit.

What is worse? Blood and feathers covering a waking toddler or a severed bird head by his cookie and a headless bird body behind him?

I opted that it would freak him out more to see the head. So I took a deep breath and picked up the warm head, cookie and bird body and tossed all three into the garbage. I remember thinking that the bird was much bigger than I had

thought. I then gently wiped my brother off. I picked feathers out of his hair. He continued to stir but I think Barbra continued to soothe him and he stayed asleep. I unbuckled and removed him from his seat. I carried him into the house.

After I woke him up I told him that Santa had called and had told me that he had to take a bath. I also told him that, if he was a good boy, Santa might chat with him on the phone! Oh boy! Roy couldn't wait for the bath!

I cleaned my baby brother. Put him in a new pair of shorts and a little Mr T muscle shirt. I placed him in his TV pillow/chair thing and turned on cartoons. As I unwrapped a new pack of cigarettes Roy began to scream.

"Santa! Santa!"

"Sorry! You took too long in the bath tub. Santa is too busy to talk!"

Classic Roy temper tantrum. I left him screaming. I walked to my car. A true shit-mobile filled with feathers and bird blood.

I lit up a cig. Smoked it down and started the process of cleaning the back seat. Again.

Only a small stain remained. I figured it sort of went well with Mr. Cohen's brain stain.

DANCING ALL THIS MESS AROUND

Stacie liked to pretend that she was from Planet Claire...

A few of our friends thought this strange, but to me it was just perfect and probably true. She barged into my life early

into my first month or so of sixth grade. Looking back, it is a miracle that she didn't drag me down the sad road she chose for herself.

My father banged on my door to tell me that there was some girl on the phone for me. I had been staring at the Texas history book I was being required to read. I had actually been planning my escape from that shitty town, my father and my life. I was dreaming of Manhattan and roaming the streets with Debbie Harry and Iggy Pop. But all of this was pushed to the back of my mind when I picked up the phone, waited for my father to hang up on his end and was greeted by hyper girlie voice singing "Planet Claire"

I lay on my bed and listened to this odd girl singing one of my favorite songs. She was totally out of tune but I was impressed that anyone actually liked the song besides me. She sang the entire song. Then there was silence.

I asked if I knew her. She said no. I asked her why she had my number and why she sung a B52's song instead of saying a simple "hello." I don't really remember how I phrased those first questions, but I am fairly certain that I didn't let on that I thought it had been funny and rather cool. I was holding my cards. But, I do remember exactly how she answered these questions.

"I got your number because I heard you have weed and like cool music. I love weed. I love cool music. Me and my friend want you to come over here and get stoned with us. She's from Jasper. I'm from Planet Claire. I don't have any money, but you will love me."

She was right. No homework was done that night. We sat under a bridge by a drainage ditch, smoked a lot of pot, talked and Stacie had her boombox blasting B52's and Pretenders. I would later turn her on to Patti Smith Group, Led Zep and Stevie Nicks. But that night it was all about new wave and bonding. Stacie demanded a lot of her friends. She was

unpredictable, prone to doing odd things just to get reactions and fearless. She expected her friends to be the same and she could care less what anyone thought of her. I loved Stacie. For the duration of middle school and high school we would remain friends even when no one else would have anything to do with her.

I enjoyed it when she would show up at the donut/snow cone shop at which I was employed. Typically, she would get in line. I'd be selling donuts to trailer park trash while the shop owners were in the back doing the "real" business of the shop, drug dealing.

The shop was a front. I was too young to work, but I was paid under the table and had easy access to dope. Interestingly, the donuts were quite popular in this very bad part of town. Stacie would always find a ride there. As she would approach the counter she would start to make odd noises. The other folks in line would try not to stare. Sometimes an older person would ask her if she was OK. If that happened the whole scene went much faster.

Stacie's odd noise making would be followed by odd jerking motions of her impossibly thin body. Her blonde hair, teased to look like Bette Midler's from THE ROSE (her favorite movie) would shake as much as her ass as she fell to the dirty floor spazzing out. The reactions would always vary. And, of course, this is what made these little planned moments from Stacie so interesting.

Most could never quite decide if she was really having an attack or if she was screwing around. Watching my customers scurry out of her way was the funniest thing about the whole sick act. There would always be some caring soul screaming at me to call an ambulance. At that point, I would normally take a couple of donuts and toss them at her face advising that she just needed sugar. Mouths would drop. Stacie would stop, examine one of the donuts shove it into her mouth and, in a completely calm tone would thank me. She would then stand

up, spit the chewed donut out and say in an almost robotic voice, "Matthew. Fuck me. Fuck me, now. Fuck me hard."

Most of the customers would leave in a state of confusion. We would start to laugh. My boss, Lynda, would emerge from the back and be so amused that she would insist I give Stacie as many donuts as she wanted.

Stacie would eventually be hired to work with me. However, it was a short span of employment for Stacie as she grew fond of messing up customers snow cones by mixing all flavors of the pure syrups without any dilution. She kept this horror in a hidden bottle under a counter light panel. If she didn't like the way a customer looked, behaved or smelled she would douse the shaved ice with this thick and sickening goop. We were children. To her, it was funny. To Lynda it was poor customer service. Spazzing out on the floor was OK, dealing drugs from the back of the store was OK, but making a customer puke was just wrong. Lynda was not amused.

In the summer of 1987, I was clean. No longer (or seldom) partaking in any drugs other than a *sometimes* toke. By this time, Stacie had gone from one addiction to another. The oddest addiction was to religion. Stacie went on a strange Jesus-trip which one could never be sure was for real or a for a joke. If I cornered her and asked for an explanation of any odd action or turn of personality she would always whisper, "I'm from Planet Claire, baby."

After she got over her Jesus/Holy Roller phase, she confessed that she had deflowered every Pentecostal and Baptist boy in our town. She told me that she liked to do this in the church on Saturday nights. The Jesus Freak Phase ended because the minister's wife and a Church Elder walked into the church late one night to discover Stacie "doing" the minister's son. She told them that she thought she was possessed by the devil. Oddly, they believed her. An exorcism was performed the next day. She didn't enjoy it as much as she thought she might. She walked out as soon as she faked

speaking in tongues. This was one of Stacie's favorite stories.

In the fall of 1987, Stacie was back into drugs, sex and rock-n-roll. I was ambivalent, in my opinion, about her situation. I loved her. I worried for her, but I didn't feel I could pass any sort of judgment. Actually, I am not one to judge people. At least, I like to pretend this is the case.

Stacie had called me up out of the blue. She asked if I could take she and a girlfriend to the beach. She wanted the three of us to spend the night talking and listening to the waves. I remember thinking that I didn't want to hang for that long because I feared I would fall back into that cycle of addiction. At this time I was seeing a shrink and was trying prescribed meds to stay clear of pot and Valium, my drug of choice at the time. But, I wanted to see Stacie and I was cool with driving them to the beach, if they thought that they could get back on their own. She told me that would be no big deal. They would just hitch a ride back the next day.

I drove to the address Stacie gave me. It was a nice home in a very nice area of our town. However, once I walked into the house I was nearly knocked out by the strong scent of weed, ammonia and body odor. There were 3 Harleys in the living room. I believe those were the only furnishings I noticed aside from some boxes. The house was full of fat, tattooed Hell's Angels types. I told this scary looking guy that I was there to pick up Stacie and her friend. He gestured down the hall and yelled, "Honey! You got a visitor!"

I stepped over a nude girl who was either sleeping, passed out or dead. My instincts told me to run, but I wanted to see Stacie. So, I called her name and she came bounding down the hall toward me. Her hair was long and straight now. She jumped on me. Her legs wrapped around my waist. She couldn't have weighed more than 90 lbs.

Her surly lesbian pal came walking up behind her. Stacie introduced her as Bull Dyke. I didn't like her. As we drove out

of the neighborhood, the Bull Dyke told me that I was cool because I turned Stacie on to Stevie Nicks and that if anyone ever tried to cut Stevie down she would take them down, but for good. Charming, but loyal.

Stacie asked if I could stop by this package store on our way. Bull Dyke wanted to pick up some beer and whiskey for the beach. No problem. I pulled in and Bull Dyke got out. Stacie laid her head on my lap and started telling me that she had decided she needed to get her shit together like me. I told her that my shit was a work in progress. I remember she laughed. She asked after a couple of former friends who no longer would talk with her. She told me that she thought she might want to go to college like me. She had all of these plans. She was talking like a junkie. I felt ill.

Bull got in the car holding a large sack. I asked her if she had gotten me a wine cooler like I had asked.

"Drive. Now. Fast!"

I followed her orders. Bull Dyke was acting funny and demanded that Stacie light up a joint for us. She refused to give me anything to drink. Stacie told me it was for the beach and I would have to stay if I wanted a cooler. Bull Dyke then called me a silly faggot for drinking pussy shit like wine coolers.

I wasn't going to screw with Stacie's new friend. I drove them to the beach. The sun was starting to set. I had given in and the three of us had a decent buzz going on. Bull Dyke was still being a bitch, but the mellow feeling of my high made it okay. Stacie begged me to stay the night. I declined and left them standing on the road leading to the water. I watched Stacie in my rear view as I drove away. She looked so sad and lost to me. But, I knew I couldn't do anything about it. She needed to do whatever it was she was doing. That was her way.

It was the fall of 1988. Stacie had been missing for well over 8 months. Her mom and sister presumed her to be dead. I just figured she was on a junkie holiday. Then, one day, I got a collect call from the state penitentiary. It was Stacie.

She had run off to Houston, got hooked on H, had been turning tricks and in an angry fit tried to murder a pimp. She shot him several times, but failed to kill him. That was her saving grace. It was only attempted murder. She explained that she had gotten off easy with just six years and expected to make parole within three.

She could only talk for a short time. She wanted to "level with me" and "get it right" because she was going to make a new start and get her shit together after she got out. She lost track of what she was going to tell me and went on and on about all sorts of post prison grand plans. Stacie was still talking like a junkie in need of a fix. She stopped talking for a few seconds, then told me she loved me and that she had to get off the phone. I asked her if she could tell me whatever it was that needed to be leveled.

"Oh, yeah. Remember that day you drove me and Bull Dyke to the beach?"

How could I forget?

"Well, we robbed that store. I was so worried about you driving back into town in that car. Bull had used a gun and I was so worried you were going to take the shit for that one. Guess we all lucked out."

The phone went dead. Her time was up. I was sort of surprised to discover that I had unknowingly taken part in a felony. But, then what could I expect? Stacie was from Planet Claire.

CONVERSATION WITH A STRIPPER

I took a break from my job search this afternoon...

...and hung out in the Haight. Ended up having a chocolate crepe for lunch at this little place near the corner of Haight and

Ashbury.

It is kind of neat to walk along the street where hippie legends were made but it is also kind of a bummer to look at all the leftover hippies who look so lost and all the rich college kids trying to pretend to be hippies. Plus, it smells of cheap booze, piss, incense and skunk-weed. But, I do like the old homes there. Tried to remember which house Janis Joplin lived in. Asked a kid who was on the street with me and he wasn't sure, but he did point out the Hendrix house.

After reading Tuesday's newspaper, I decided to head back home. I had walked all the way from the piers to the edge of Tenderloin to have tea at this cool little café. It was cold and looked like it might rain at any minute so I opted to take the bus back to the underground MUNI (AKA subway) to head back to Ingleside. I do not like riding the busses. I am a magnet for oddness and it seems that they are often filled with the odd stench of mothballs and body odor, but this would be a short ride and I had my iPod.

The bus stop is not too far from one of the many strip clubs in the city. Though seedy, this club has a kind of cool vibe about it. You get the feeling that in a few years these places will most likely be nothing more than a memory. To many, I think that is a good thing, but I kind of like knowing that seedy isn't too far away.

I stood there staring off into space milling a million thoughts through my head with the Chronicle clutched in my left hand and iPod in my right. I hadn't turned it on yet. I like to be fully aware of what is going on around me when in these areas of town.

I caught a scent of nice perfume and then a smoky voice asked, "Any good news, baby?"

I turned. It was a pretty woman of color with her hair pinned up, an interesting sort of sweater coat, a huge purse

and massive black boots with spike heels.

"No, just the same old bad news. Do you want it? I'm all done," I answered.

She smiled and told me she liked the horoscope and the sports sections. She took it with thanks. We stood there waiting for the bus. She sighed.

"So, sweetie, what time is it anyway?"

I looked my watch and told her it was 3:45. She sighed again. I could feel her looking at me, but I liked the way she smelled. So, since she was looking at me I asked, "You have a great scent. What are you wearing?"

She laughed. "I knew it. You're a gay boy. I just couldn't decide. Thanks. I borrowed a few sprays on my way out. I was worried I stunk."

I smiled, "Well, I'm queer but hardly a boy. I love you for calling me a boy, though!"

She laughed and told me that gay dudes stay younger than straight guys. She then said something about how she wished straight guys would start to copy gay boys more. She then told me that her boots were killing her and that she had been dancing for hours. I am a little slow on the pick up, but it struck me that she must have just come out of the seedy little strip joint/bar.

"Do you dance?" I asked, pointing to the establishment.

And, her answer amused me, but not in a comical way. She answered by saying, "Dancing? Well, I guess you could call it that. I gave up on the idea of being a dancer years ago. It's a living."

We both turned as we heard the bus approaching. A

suspect looking guy sort of came out of nowhere and walked up to her. He mumbled something and she seemed to be ignoring him. I started toward the bus door, but she stayed in place. I looked and the guy had her arm. He was whispering to her and she looked annoyed. Probably not too smart of me, but I asked, "Are you okay?"

And she smiled at me and nodded to indicate she was cool. I got on the bus. I bent down and watched as the bus pulled away. She was turning and walking back toward the bar with the guy.

I turned on my iPod.

How much is a choice and how much is a trap? When does something turn from being an act of liberation to an act of desperation? Did she hate that man or was that an act on her part for his benefit? And, why would you elect to wear dominatrix like boots after dancing for hours?

Some dance music came on the iPod. I closed my eyes and imagined that lady dancing to the song. I wondered what her name was. I hoped it was "Trixie."

THE CAPTAIN & TENNILLE,
MOM AND MY FIRST ERECTION

December 27th, 1976. I had just turned 10...

 It was after dinner from What-A-Burger. My cassette tape
of A STAR IS BORN was playing. My mom has been dancing to

"Queen Bee" and I decided to tell her about a concern of mine. I told her that my penis got big and I was afraid it was going to explode. She had asked me what I was thinking when my "penis became erect." Erect was a new word for me. I remember thinking it had something to do with Kris Kristofferson's chest and beard, but I told her I didn't know.

After the song ended, she sat down on my bed and had me sit next to her. There was a poster of The Captain & Tennille on my wall. I think this was from the cover of "The Song of Joy" LP. I loved The Captain & Tennille.

The conversation/sex lesson went like this:

Mom: "You probably got excited when you saw Barbra Streisand's breasts getting touched by Kris Kristofferson. I liked seeing Kris Kristofferson do that to her, too. You see, when adult's get naked together, they get excited. For a grown up woman that can sometimes mean that her vagina gets very moist. Sometimes a vagina can get wet.

"Wet?"

"Now, a grown-up man's penis swells up and gets hard when he gets excited. Do you know why?"

I didn't, but I knew she was about to tell me. Funny, my mother was always so open about sex but that just made me all the more uncomfortable when she talked about it.

"Because he wants to put his erect penis into the moist vagina."

"What?"

"You know I explained this to you before when your Dad took you to see that scary move."

"You mean CARRIE or THE TEXAS CHAINSAW MASSACRE?" (I then pronounced it as "*mass-a-cree.*")

"CARRIE. Your father took you to see that chainsaw movie? I didn't know that. Well, look" as she pointed to The Captain. "When The Captain sees Tennille naked, he sometimes gets excited or turned on. When that happens his penis gets bigger and hard. Like yours did today." Now, she was pointing to Tennille.

"When The Captain is naked and his penis is big and hard, Tennille gets excited and her vagina gets very wet and The Captain puts his erect penis into Tennille's vagina."

"He puts his penis inside her?"

"Yes. And he does this over and over again until both he and Tennille get so excited that his penis spurts sperm into Tennille. That is how they can make a baby. Because one of his sperm can sometimes meet her egg which is located inside Tennille's vagina..."

"There's an egg in Tennille?"

"Well, a very tiny egg. There is one in me, too. There is one in every grown up woman. Remember? I explained about that ugly girl in CARRIE? Why she was bleeding?"

"No."

"I could ask your daddy to talk to you, but I don't like the way he says things. Do you want me to draw you some pictures?"

"Does The Captain pee in Tennille?"

My progressive mother was clearly getting annoyed. "No, sperm is not the same as pee! When The Captain's penis gets hard he can't pee. He can only ejaculate sperm. Do you

understand?"

I just wanted my mother to leave.

"Yes," I answered.

"Good! Wanna dance to some Abba? That Barbra Streisand hurts my ears!"

"No."

She leaves.

I hear Abba singing from the living room.

I look at my poster of The Captain & Tennille.

Later that night, I take it down. And, I never hear them without thinking of this discussion. To this day, my mother denies any memory of using them as her example. But, in what feels like a form of diversion, she drifts off and starts telling me how much she loves the song where Tennille sings, "Got-cha!"

FURTHER ADVENTURES AT THE FREE CLINIC

I had no choice but to return...

... to the free clinic in that scary ass part of the city. However, as always, I kind of enjoy the experience. I can

lament on and on about the odd luck of my life but I will never claim my life is dull. It is interesting. After a day full of faux drama at my wondrous big fat gay job, I left 2 hours early to head to the clinic. If my bosses and co-workers saw where I had to go I am certain that they would break the rules and just give me insurance now. I guess bumping from job to job presents certain challenges I must face.

After letting them inspect my messenger bag to ensure I was packing no heat, knives or PNP supplies and signing in, I took my seat. So, there I was. Me, 4 street workers clearly in need of some meth, crack or H, several insane homeless men and an interesting woman who we will call "Ida."

Ida was my friend for the three hours I was there. We chatted. She tried to cut her hair. She told me it was too long and matted. However, much to my relief, one of the guards came and took Ida's shears away. Actually, they were not really shears. They were little elementary school scissors. She was upset about not being able to style her hair while she waited.

"Ida. Shut the fuck up!" an exasperated crack addict bellowed after Ida continued to complain to me that her hair was in need of "some work.'" Before an argument broke out and the crazy dude to our left started crying again, a lady at the front desk announced that it was time for Oprah. A wave of excitement swept over the room as Gladys got up and changed the channel to Oprah. It was an electric moment!

For the next 30 minutes or so we watched Oprah explain that we were all living beyond our means. Oprah never mentioned that her outfit probably cost as much as the annual budget for the free clinic and I swear it looked as if someone was changing her hair between commercial breaks.

"Poor thing. She's got all that money and the bitch still can't do her hair," so spoke the wisdom of Ida. Hair seemed to be heavy on Ida's mind today.

Anyway, as Ida went on and on about Oprah's set, which, Ida felt was too brown. Actually, she had a point or it might have been the poor reception of the TV. I decided to pull out my journal and write all of this magic moment down so I could share it with you because that is what I am all about.

"Hey, Matt-Boy, I like your bag!" Ida announced as she gently stroked it.

"Thanks. It works" I replied.

"Can I have it?" she asked.

"No" I answered.

One of the crazy men started laughing. Ida reached over and slapped his head. I am not sure if the hair cutting or the slap caused it, but Ida got to see the doctor before me. We never saw her leave.

The doctor saw me for all of three minutes. He asked me how my day was going and refilled my two meds which I can't wait to stop taking but will have to get a doctor to do so. Then I signed out, walked to BART and headed home.

The sun has returned. As has that wonderful San Francisco breeze. I love the way it feels. I sat out in A's backyard when I got home. I wonder if Oprah would be nice to me and Ida if we went on her show. Ida could get a makeover and Oprah could teach me how to better budget and set me up on a date.

Well, a boy can dream.

HOT FOR TEACHER

There were too many "bad" kids at my junior high...

I went to the "poor" one in my hometown. The nicer one was on Phelan Blvd. Mine was on some creepy side street...

the name of which I've long since forgotten.

Anyway, during my 8th grade year, the school faced the challenge of finding a way to fit all of us "bad" kids into detention. Sitting us on the floor wasn't working. Most of us would nap. So, our lame principal came up with the ever-clever idea of post-modern behavior modification. In his eyes, poetry was equal to punishment. So, lesser offenses would actually merit a Punishment Choice for the offender: for girls, you could choose to memorize a poem or run 8 laps after school; for boys, you could choose between poetry memorization, ten laps or ten "licks" from Coach Mendozola.

The guys lived in mortal fear of Coach Mendozola's spankings or "licks." Coach Mendozola was a stocky but hot Latino guy who probably opted to become a teacher because he could get summers off. He was about 6 foot and 200 pounds of pure hairy muscle. And, he seemed to take a sick sort of pleasure in spanking the boys.

"Mr. Stanfield, we have advised you that smoking is not allowed on campus. Normally, you would be sent straight to detention, but now you have to make a choice. What will it be?"

A four second pause...

"Um, well, er, I guess I'll just take the licks."

Gasps from my fellow students in the principal's office waiting area.

Fast forward to 3:30 PM. I am in Coach Mendozola's little office located off the side of the stinky boys shower/dressing area. He always managed to leave his "Playboy" magazine sitting out on his desk to taunt the boys. I still don't know how he avoided getting into trouble. But, this was 1982 and our Junior High Baseball team was always scoring touchdowns or some such. Or, was it basketball? I don't know from sports.

Anyway, it would usually play out like this...

"Stanfield. You again? You better get it together, son or you're headed for a heap of trouble."

"Yes, sir."

My every pore was beating with anticipation.

"Well, son. OK, let's go."

I would follow Coach M out into the boys' dressing area. It smelled of sweat, bleach and that pseudo man-scent. There was the bench we sat on to put on or take off our shoes/socks. Coach M would motion to the bench, his paddle in hand.

"Get down and bend over the bench. You know the drill."

"Yes, sir"

I got down and bent myself over the bench.

Wham! Wham! Wham! Wham! Wham! Wham! Wham!

"Are you going to smoke anymore, Stanfield?"

...Smiling on the inside in more ways than one, "No, sir!"

Wham! Wham! Wham!

My butt was stinging but I was in love. I stood up.

"You know, Stanfield..." Coach M was cradling his warm paddle and looking at me with those intense brown eyes, "You really should just start dipping. You won't get in trouble. I don't blame you for taking the licks, though. Who wants to memorize a fucking poem, huh? Dumb shits. They're all

pussies. I'd take a lickin' any day over that crap."

"Yes, sir."

"OK. Get out here. I got some reading to do."

Not that I was into getting spanked or anything....

GERMS

Today was my last visit to the free clinic for my meds...

At least I hope it was. My insurance goes into effect next month. This is a good thing because today was my worst visit

yet.

When I walked in, I was surprised to discover that there were only two people waiting and both seemed to be fairly grounded. I signed in and chatted with the guard. I confirmed I had no weapons or sharp objects in my bag and confirmed that this should be my last visit.

I took a seat in the front row. The TV was screening The Tyra Banks Show. Normally, I have to spend a great deal of time at the clinic per visit. I had brought a book of short stories to fill the time, but I found myself drawn into the hazy dew of Tyra's program. She was doing a show on germs. Tyra and her guests were discussing concerns regarding public and private places, the sorts of germs one can encounter in these spaces and what are the best options one can take to protect your system from being attacked by these gruesome germ creatures.

It was actually interesting. I learned that when one has to use a public toilet, one should always go to the first stall because it gets more air and is the least used of the stalls. I also learned that toilet seats carry fewer germs than the average household kitchen sponge. And urine is fairly sterile and of little concern when it comes to germs. In addition, any pesky germs that might be in piss die as soon as the spray jets off into air.

According to Tyra and her panel of experts, the best option is to wipe the toilet seat and sit down. No need to worry with those wax paper toilet seat covers or trying to place toilet paper over the seat because there is a stronger danger of encountering germs when your hands are doing such things. Also, when washing your hands, it is important to lather up and wash for a minimum of 20 seconds.

The talk show continued to teach me things I had not known before. Apparently, according to Tyra, the average human carries a surprising amount of fecal matter in his/her

underwear. It is very bad to wear underwear more than once without washing. And, it is even worse to not wear underwear. Going natural is not a good germ choice. Also quite surprising was the revelation that germ passing via use of public toilets, hotels beds and shaking hands should be of minor concern when compared to the horrid nightmare that is the common kitchen sponge. And, the hidden germ dangers of your kitchen!

Tyra explained with great enthusiasm that sponges should be washed daily and placed in the microwave for approximately one minute after being washed. It was all quite interesting. A microscope revealed that a sponge could be the host to Alien-like creatures that made me squirm in my chair. Then, as an added bonus, Tyra began to demonstrate how she uses public toilets! It was at this point that my safe and germ-free world of model-presented TV was shattered with the following exclamation:

"I'm gonna fuckin' cut you, muthafucka!"

I looked to my left and discovered an obviously off-balance man welding what looked like a sort of makeshift knife. It was a yellow toothbrush with a razor blade attached by twine. I would later learn that this is called a "shiv." He emitted a stench of piss, vomit and whiskey. He was all twitchy and angry. I could see the guard sneaking up from behind to grab him. The guard was also pressing some red button on the wall. Up until that moment I thought things like this only happened in bad Linda Blair movies.

Let's call my new *friend* with the shiv 'Randy.'

"'Randy,' honey, take a deep breath and drop the knife. *Everything is okay.* No one here is going to hurt you," so spoke one of the nice folks behind the counter.

"YOU'RE DAMN FUCKIN' RIGHT NO ONE IS EVER GONNA HURT MY MUTHAFUCKIN' ASS AGAIN!! I'M GONNA CUT YOU DEEP, BITCH!"

I could hear the two people behind me getting up. It sounded like one was running toward the hallway behind us that led to the doctors we were waiting to see.

'Randy' sort of twitched forward closer to me and screamed, *"WHERE THE FUCK YOU GOIN' MUTHAFUCKA? STAY HERE! I WANT YOUR WALLET, ASSHOLE!"*

I no longer heard running.

"'Randy,' now *think* about what you're doing. *Drop the blade* and everything will be okay."

And then, 'Randy' looked at me.

"'Randy' come on. Drop the knife and Joe will come out and talk to you and make everything okay."

But, 'Randy' seemed to have adopted the single purpose of looking at me.

"GIVE ME YOUR PURSE! I WANT YOUR PURSE!"

First of all, I feel duty bound to explain that it was a messenger bag. At worst, it might be considered a man bag. Well, I guess you could call it a man purse or possibly a *murse*. Why lie to you? Okay. It is a purse and it contains my whole universe.

"NO FUCK OFF!" I screeched in my most 'butch' voice.

Yeah, this is what I said to a mentally unhinged psycho with a shiv pointed toward me.

"MUTHAFUCKA GIVE ME THAT FUCKIN' PURSE!"

"NO FUCKING WAY!"

I found myself holding my way-cool bag close to my person like a baby. In this highly fashionable bag were my mini iPod, my meds, my chewing gum, my keys, my cell phone, my Hello Kitty note pad and my passport. No way this fucker was going to take my murse. I was getting ready to kick. Luckily, I was wearing my Doc Martens and not my new way cool gay pink sneakers.

"'Randy' he is going to give you his bag, but you need to drop the knife"

It was at this point that I realized I was probably being a wee bit stupid. And yet, I stayed poised ready to kick. My legs up, my feet pointed out toward 'Randy' and my bag pressed firmly against my chest. I was Tyra-ready to jump this psycho. You know, maybe not as powerful as Oprah, but a hell of a lot meaner!

Luckily, the guard and three other guys who had been creeping up behind 'all pounced upon him and took him to the ground. A lady came running from behind the counter with a syringe in her latex gloved hand and shoved it into his shoulder. 'Randy' was down for the count and the shiv was on the floor a few feet away from him. Another lady picked up the scary knife. She, too, was wearing gloves.

Germs.

Sirens, some cops, a restraining jacket and bound to a stretcher, and 'Randy' was carried out and away.

I had been at the clinic for only about 30 minutes thus far. I was bumped ahead of my two fellow patients. I was led to a private space. As he wrote out my two prescriptions he

lectured me on the fact that you never agitate someone like I had and that nothing was worth putting my life or the lives of others at risk. I apologized and told him it was sort of automatic.

He rolled his eyes. His hands were still trembling. I was surprisingly calm. I took the slips of paper and he told me to be well. He wished me luck with my new job and on getting off the meds. I left with my purse and contents in tact. I picked up a vanilla malt and headed home on the M-train.

As interesting as my little adventure for the day had been, nothing can compare to seeing Tyra Banks demonstrate how she takes a dump.